For Billy

ALADDIN

An imprint of Simon & Schuster Children's Publishing Division
1230 Avenue of the Americas, New York, New York 10020
This Aladdin hardcover edition May 2018
Text and illustrations copyright © 2012 by Sue Hendra
By Paul Linnet and Sue Hendra
Originally published in Great Britain in 2012 by Simon & Schuster UK Ltd
Published by arrangement with Simon & Schuster UK Ltd
For information about special discounts for bulk purchases,
please contact Simon & Schuster Special Sales at 1-866-506-1949
or business@simonandschuster.com.
The Simon & Schuster Speakers Bureau can bring authors to
your live event. For more information or to book an event contact
the Simon & Schuster Speakers Bureau at 1-866-248-3049 or
visit our website at www.simonspeakers.com.
The text of this book was set in Happyjamas.
Manufactured in China 0218 SCP
2 4 6 8 10 9 7 5 3 1
Library of Congress Control Number 2017945986
ISBN 978-1-4814-9035-1 (hc)
ISBN 978-1-4814-9036-8 (eBook)

KEITH
THE CAT WITH THE MAGIC HAT

by Sue Hendra

ALADDIN
New York   London   Toronto   Sydney   New Delhi

Keith the cat was merrily minding
his own business when . . .

"Ha-ha-ha, Keith's got ice cream stuck on his head!" chuckled the other cats.

Suddenly, Keith felt a little bit shy and a little bit silly.

"It's not ice cream," he squeaked. "It's a . . .

It's a . . .

It's a . . .

It's a . . .

MAGIC HAT!
Yes, that's it!
A MAGIC HAT!"

This made the other cats laugh even louder.
"Go on, then. Show us some magic!" they chortled.

Poor Keith! What was he going to do?
"W-w-well, first," stammered Keith,
"I need my magic wand."

He reached for the chocolatey magic
wand on the ground but . . .

It started to run away—
ALL by itself!

The cats were amazed.
"Wow, Keith! You made
it move," they gasped.

Keith was amazed too . . . but he didn't say anything.
"More!" the cats cried excitedly.
"More magic. More! More!"

Keith took a deep breath.
Then he waved his wand around . . .

"Abracadabra!"

But nothing happened.

Keith tried again.

"Alacazoo!"

Still nothing happened.

The cats were getting impatient.
They chanted and stamped their feet.
"MORE! MORE! MORE!"
"Whizzy-whoo-do-da!"
cried Keith AND . . . .

. . . just then, a whole family of rabbits popped out of the ground. They'd never heard such a noise!

"Keith—you did it!" the other cats cheered.
"You magicked up some rabbits. Hooray!"

They were all having such a fun time
that they didn't hear a distant WOOF!

WOOF! WOOF! WOOF!

"Yikes! A dog! Quick, Keith, save us with your magic!" the cats squealed in panic.

WOOF! WOOF! WOOF!

But, of course, Keith couldn't REALLY do magic.
What was he going to do?

The cats ran up the tree.

They looked down at the barking dog. "Quick, Keith, do something!" they cried.

Then . . .

Whoops!

Keith's magic hat slipped off his head.
It was falling quickly through the air . . .

"Oh no! Your magic hat!" cried the cats.
"Now you'll NEVER be able to make
the dog disappear."

Keith felt terrible.
"It's not a magic hat," he admitted sadly.
"You were right all along—it's just ice cream,
and now we are stuck up this tree FOREVER!
I'm sorry!"

But then . . .

"Hooray for Keith!" cried the cats.
"You're magic even without your hat!"
"Thank you," said Keith shyly. "And, for my
next trick, I will make this blob of ice cream
on the end of my nose disappear."

The cats waited patiently.

Then . . .

Keith stuck out his tongue and licked it off!